This Walker book belongs to:

_____

_____

_____

For Helen with love
S.H.

For Christle, Mimi, Ruth and Didi
H.C.

First published 1986 by Walker Books Ltd,
87 Vauxhall Walk, London SE11 5HJ

This edition published 2011

2 4 6 8 10 9 7 5 3 1

Text © 1986 Sarah Hayes
Illustrations © 1986 Helen Craig Ltd

The right of Sarah Hayes and Helen Craig to be identified as author
and illustrator respectively of this artwork has been asserted by them
in accordance with the Copyright, Designs and Patents Act 1988

This book has been typeset in Garamond

Printed in China

British Library Cataloguing in Publication Data:
a catalogue record for this book is available from the British Library

ISBN 978-1-4063-3484-5

www.walker.co.uk

THIS IS THE
BEAR

AND THE
PICNIC LUNCH

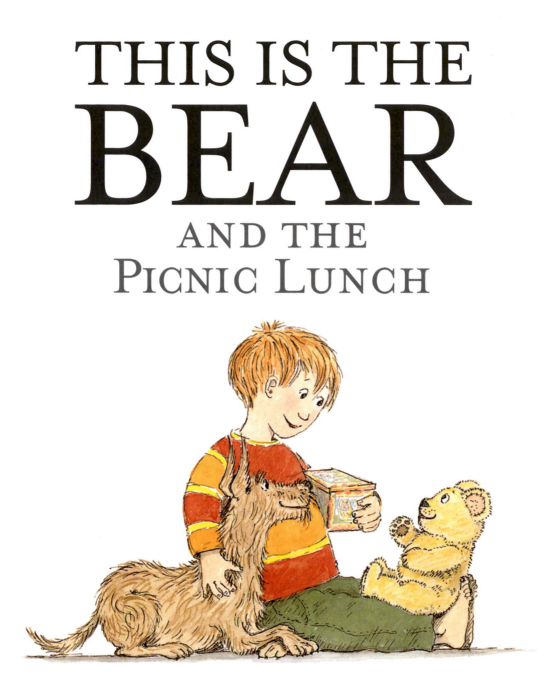

SARAH HAYES

ILLUSTRATED BY HELEN CRAIG

WALKER BOOKS

AND SUBSIDIARIES

LONDON • BOSTON • SYDNEY • AUCKLAND

This is the boy

who packed a lunch

of sandwiches, crisps and
an apple to crunch.

This is the bear
who guarded the box

while the boy went to find
his shoes and socks.

This is the dog
who sneaked past the chair

towards the lunch and
the brave guard bear.

This is the bear
with his eyes half closed
who did not notice
the dog's black nose.

This is the bear
who was sound asleep

when the dog performed
a tremendous leap...

on to the table…

down to the floor...

and off to hide

behind the door . . .

and all that he left
of the picnic lunch
was an empty box and
the apple to crunch.

This is the boy
who looked everywhere

for his lunch and his dog
and his brave guard bear.

This is the boy

who heard the munch

of a dog and a bear
eating picnic lunch.

This is the boy
who tried to be angry

but found he was
suddenly terribly hungry.

This is the boy
who packed a new lunch
of sandwiches, crisps and
the apple to crunch.
And this is the bear who said,
"Haven't you guessed?
Indoor picnics are the best!"

All four *This is the Bear* stories

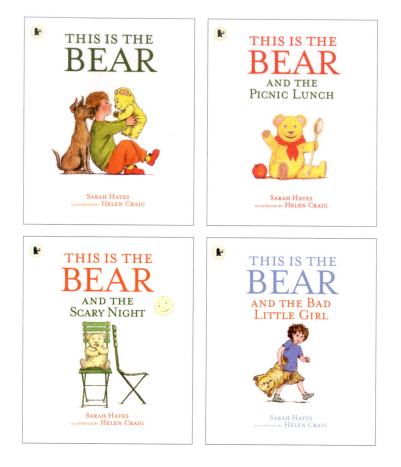

Sarah Hayes is the author of many books for children, including the *This is the Bear* quartet; *Mary, Mary*; *Happy Christmas*; and *Eat Up, Gemma* (shortlisted for the Smarties Book Prize).

Helen Craig is a widely acclaimed illustrator of books for children, whose work includes *The Town Mouse and the Country Mouse* (shortlisted for the Smarties Book Prize); *Rosie's Visitors*; and the hugely popular stories about *Angelina Ballerina*, who has featured in her own animated TV series.

www.walker.co.uk